The Cro
Of
Curly Pride

Rochelle Robertson

Once upon a time, in the vibrant city of New Orleans, lived a young boy named Jamal.

Jamal was seven years old, with a big heart and even bigger dreams.

He loved playing outside with his friends, drawing colorful pictures, and listening to his grandma's enchanting stories about their family history.

But there was one thing about Jamal that he wasn't so sure about: his hair.

His hair was curly, coily, and seemed to have a mind of its own.

Jamal often saw other kids at school with straight or wavy hair, and he wondered why his hair looked different.

One sunny afternoon, as Jamal played in the park, he noticed a little girl with beautiful braids adorned with colorful beads.

She smiled at him and said, "I love your curly hair! It looks like a crown."

Jamal blushed and thanked her, but he still felt unsure.

That night, he told his mom about his worries. She listened carefully and then led him to a large photo album filled with pictures of their family.

She pointed to a picture of a young man with a proud, radiant smile and a head full of curls.

"That's your Grandpa Samuel," she said. "He loved his hair just like you should love yours. Your hair is a part of who you are, Jamal. It's a crown that shows the world your strength and heritage."

Jamal's eyes widened as he looked at the picture. He had always admired his grandpa, who was known for his kindness and wisdom. That night, he fell asleep thinking about his grandpa's words.

The next day at school, Jamal decided to try something new. He wore his favorite hat, the one his grandpa had given him, and walked into class with a confident smile. His friends noticed right away.

"Wow, Jamal! Your hair looks amazing today," said his friend Alex.

Jamal grinned and said, "Thanks! I've decided to embrace my curls. They're a part of who I am."

As the days went by, Jamal's confidence grew. He started trying out different hairstyles and even shared some tips with his friends. He learned to love his hair for its uniqueness and realized that it was a special part of his identity.

One afternoon, Jamal's class had a "show and tell" session.

He brought in the photo album and proudly showed his classmates the picture of his grandpa. He told them about his family's history and how he had learned to love his natural hair.

His teacher smiled and said, "Jamal, thank you for sharing your story with us. It's a beautiful reminder that we should all embrace who we are, inside and out."

From that day on, Jamal felt a sense of pride in his curls. He knew that his hair was more than just curls—it was a crown, a symbol of his heritage, and a reminder to always love himself just as he was.

And so, Jamal continued to wear his curls with pride, knowing that his journey of self-love had made him stronger and more confident than ever before.

Made in the USA
Columbia, SC
26 March 2025